Katie Woo

Flower Girl Katie

by Fran Manushkin

illustrated by Tammie Lyon

PICTURE WINDOW BOOKS
a capstone imprint

Katie Woo is published by Picture Window Books,
A Capstone Imprint
1710 Roe Crest Drive
North Mankato, Minnesota 56003
www.mycapstone.com

Text © 2019 Fran Manushkin
Illustrations © 2019 Picture Window Books

Library of Congress Cataloging-in-Publication Data
Names: Manushkin, Fran, author. | Lyon, Tammie, illustrator. |
    Manushkin, Fran. Katie Woo.
Title: Flower girl Katie / by Fran Manushkin ; illustrated by Tammie Lyon.
Description: North Mankato, Minnesota : Picture Window Books, [2019] |
    Series: Katie Woo | Summary: Katie is delighted when her Aunt Patty
    asks her to be a flower girl--but then she starts thinking about
    everything that could go wrong and worries that she will spoil her
    aunt's wedding.
Identifiers: LCCN 2018038085| ISBN 9781515838425 (hardcover) | ISBN
    9781515840473 (pbk.) | ISBN 9781515838456 (ebook pdf)
Subjects: LCSH: Woo, Katie (Fictitious character)—Juvenile fiction. |
    Chinese Americans—Juvenile fiction. | Flower girls--Juvenile fiction. |
    Aunts—Juvenile fiction. | Weddings—Juvenile fiction. | CYAC: Chinese
    Americans—Fiction. | Flower girls—Fiction. | Aunts—Fiction. |
    Weddings—Fiction.
Classification: LCC PZ7.M3195 Fj 2019 | DDC 813.54 [E] —dc23
LC record available at https://lccn.loc.gov/2018038085

Graphic Designer: Bobbie Nuytten

Printed in the United States   4494

Table of Contents

Chapter 1
Wedding News

Katie loved to visit her Aunt Patty. She was very glamorous!

When they had tea parties, Katie and JoJo wore Aunt Patty's fancy hats.

One day, Aunt Patty told Katie, "I'm getting married. I want you to be my flower girl."

Katie was thrilled.

"You'll be great!" said JoJo.

At school, Mattie told

Katie, "I was a flower girl.

It can be tricky."

"How tricky can it be?"

asked JoJo.

"I can show you on

Saturday," said Mattie.

Yoko and Fatima said

they wanted to come too.

On Saturday, the girls met at Katie's house.

Mattie said, "The bride wears something old, something new, something borrowed, and something blue. You should too. It will bring your aunt luck."

"I have something old,"
said Fatima. "It's a butterfly
pin my grandma gave me."

"Thank you," said Katie.
"I will try not to lose it."

"I have something new,"
said Mattie. "My fancy socks
with lace and ruffles."

"Wow!" said Katie. "My
feet and I will be happy.
I know I can't lose them."

Yoko asked, "Would
you like to borrow my pink
headband?"

"It's perfect," said Katie.
"I'm wearing a pink dress."

"Terrific!" said JoJo. "You
look great in pink!"

Chapter 2

Feeling Nervous

"Now," said Mattie, "Katie should practice tossing flowers. Let's pretend these dandelions are rose petals."

Katie began tossing petals.

"Be sure not to drop the basket," said Yoko. "I saw a flower girl do that once."

"Oh my," said Katie.

"Katie won't!" said JoJo.

"And don't step on the bride's train," said Fatima. "Her dress could fall off."

"Oh no!" Katie groaned. "There is so much to worry about."

Katie told her mom,

"Being a flower girl is tricky.

Terrible things can happen!"

"Don't worry," said her

mom. But Katie worried.

That night, she had a
flower girl nightmare. Katie
dreamed that she tripped
and fell in the mud.

It was scary!

The next day, Katie

asked Aunt Patty, "Are you

sure you want me to be your

flower girl? I will have to be

perfect."

"You will be terrific," said

Aunt Patty.

Chapter 3
Feeling Terrific

Katie practiced walking.

She walked very carefully.

Oops! She kept tripping.

"Just walk like you

always do," said JoJo.

Katie smiled. "That's

easy."

At school, Katie said, "I forgot to borrow something blue."

"Don't worry," said JoJo. "Here's my bluebird bracelet."

Katie hugged her. "JoJo, you always save me!"

As they left school, Katie thought about JoJo. "When I'm with her, she makes me feel terrific."

Katie thought about JoJo all the way home.

That night,

Katie asked

Aunt Patty, "Can

a wedding have *two* flower

girls? If JoJo is with me, I

will feel calm. And I won't

step on your dress."

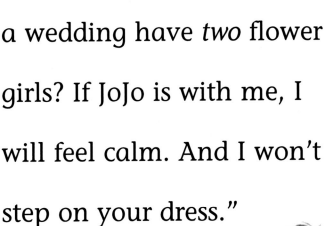

"That's a

wonderful idea,"

said Aunt Patty.

"I love JoJo."

When Katie told JoJo,

oh how they hugged!

Katie said, "It will be

twice as much fun marching

with you!"

As they tossed the rose petals, Katie said, "I feel like a princess."

"Me too!" said JoJo.

Nobody tripped, and everyone smiled.

At the party, Katie and JoJo did wild dances together.

Katie told JoJo, "Nobody is blue at this wedding."

And it was true!

About the Author

Fran Manushkin is the author of many popular picture books, including *Happy in Our Skin; Baby, Come Out!; Latkes and Applesauce: A Hanukkah Story; The Tushy Book; Big Girl Panties; Big Boy Underpants;* and *Bamboo for Me, Bamboo for You!* There is a real Katie Woo—she's Fran's great-niece—but she never gets in half the trouble of the Katie Woo in the books. Fran writes on her beloved Mac computer in New York City, without the help of her two naughty cats, Chaim and Goldy.

About the Illustrator

Tammie Lyon began her love for drawing at a young age while sitting at the kitchen table with her dad. She continued her love of art and eventually attended the Columbus College of Art and Design, where she earned a bachelor's degree in fine art. After a brief career as a professional ballet dancer, she decided to devote herself full time to illustration. Today she lives with her husband, Lee, in Cincinnati, Ohio. Her dogs, Gus and Dudley, keep her company as she works in her studio.

Glossary

dandelions (DAN-duh-lye-uhns)—plants with bright yellow flowers that are often found on lawns

glamorous (GLAM-ur-uhss)—pretty and exciting

groaned (GROHND)—made a deep, low sound to show pain or unhappiness

nightmare (NITE-mair)—a frightening or unpleasant dream

terrible (TER-uh-buhl)—very bad or unpleasant

terrific (tuh-RIF-ik)—very good or excellent

thrilled (THRILD)—very excited and happy

Let's Talk

1. In what ways did Katie's friends try to help her? Were they actually helpful? Explain your answer.

2. What do you think was the trickiest part of being a flower girl for Katie? Would you be as nervous as Katie was?

3. Explain why Katie wanted JoJo to be a flower girl too.

Let's Write

1. Pretend you are bringing something old, something new, something borrowed, and something blue for luck at a wedding. Write down what you would bring for each thing.

2. Pretend you are Katie, and make a wedding card for Aunt Patty and your new uncle. Be sure to write a special message inside.

3. Imagine that Katie gets Mattie's socks really stinky. What should Katie do? Write a paragraph.

Having Fun with Katie Woo!

Katie and JoJo love wearing Aunt Patty's fancy hats at tea parties. You can make a fancy hat of your own with supplies from around the house!

Fancy Hat Fun

What you need:

- small 2-inch foil pie tin (You can also use a small paper plate)

- bamboo skewer

- elastic cord or ribbon

- decorations such as sequins, paper doilies, pom-poms, paper cupcake liners, etc.

- craft glue

What you do:

1. Setting the pie tin upside down on your head, measure a length of elastic cord or ribbon to safely hold your hat on your head. A partner can be a great help for this step.

2. Using the bamboo skewer, poke two small holes in the bottom of the pie tin, one on each side. Thread the cord or ribbon through the holes, and tie secure knots that are big enough that they won't pull back through the hole.

3. Now use all your decorations to jazz up the top of your tin any way you would like! To make paper flowers, glue a pom-pom in the center of a cupcake liner. Wouldn't a hat full of paper flowers be pretty?

THE FUN DOESN'T STOP HERE!

Discover more at www.capstonekids.com

♡ Videos & Contests

✿ Games & Puzzles

♡ Friends & Favorites

✿ Authors & Illustrators

Find cool websites and more books like this one at www.facthound.com. Just type in the Book ID: **9781515838425** and you're ready to go!

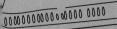